For Theo + Rosa.
                    —G. R.

For Ann D. Woodward with love.
Thank you for being such a good friend!
                                —C. H.

In the New World

A Family in Two Centuries

Gerda Raidt • Christa Holtei

■■■ Charlesbridge

The Journey into a New World

In the 1850s, large numbers of people in Germany began to leave their home country to seek a new life in America. In some cases entire villages decided to emigrate together. By the end of the century, nearly six million Germans had settled in the United States.

One reason Germans decided to move away was a lack of food. Because doctors had made progress with treating once-deadly diseases, Germany had twice as many inhabitants as only fifty years before. The harvests could no longer feed everyone. Powerful storms and pests also took their toll on crops. Grain and potatoes cost twice as much as they had before.

Many people couldn't afford such high prices. Peasant farmers, craftsmen, and wage laborers had the hardest time. They had been able to support themselves by selling homemade goods, but now more and more products were produced—quickly and cheaply—by machines in factories. People didn't think their families would survive if they stayed in their homeland.

Today more than fifty million Americans are descended from Germans, making it the largest ancestral group in the United States. City names such as Bingen (in Washington), Hanover (in Pennsylvania), Muenster (in Texas), Karlsruhe (in North Dakota), and Augsburg (in Arkansas) reflect this lineage.

Most Americans of German descent speak no German at all. Some, however, not only speak German fluently but have also preserved their regional dialect. Many are curious about their origins and why their ancestors chose to leave home.

Let's take a closer look at an immigrant family's journey. It begins in the spring of 1869 in a small village in the Prussian province of Hanover, in the home of Robert and Margarete Peters and their two children: Johannes, who is eight, and Dorothea, who is six.

Johannes   Robert   Margarete   Dorothea
(John)   (Bob)   (Maggy)   (Dotty)

1869: Difficult Decisions

At Home in the Village

Robert Peters is a peasant farmer and linen weaver. He lives with his family on a farm in a timber-frame house. He also has a barn with stalls for livestock, a few chickens, and a field behind the house.

Robert's parents had a lot of land, but the law required them to divide it up among Robert and his brothers and sisters, just as Robert's grandparents had done for their children. Now Robert has only a tiny plot, not enough for a good grain harvest.

Not Enough to Live On

Robert and Margarete plant flax in the field. In autumn and winter the family processes the flax, and Margarete spins thread from the fibers. Robert spends long hours sitting at his loom, weaving the thread into linen fabric. He sells it to be made into clothing, bedding, book binding, and painters' canvases. Robert used to be able to keep his family afloat with his trade, but not anymore. Robert and Margarete are worried.

Deciding to Start Over?

Robert has seen in the newspaper that there is plenty of land in America. More and more people are moving to the United States, and they need goods: food, clothing, homes, and furniture. Anyone skilled in farming or handicrafts can make a good living.

It takes a long time for Robert and Margarete to decide to move. They know it won't be easy to leave their home and give up almost everything they have ever owned.

A photographer takes a souvenir picture. The Peters family auctions off their belongings: livestock, loom, house, and furniture. The children even have to give up their favorite goose, Gundula.

Margarete and Dorothea sew cloth sacks to carry provisions for their journey.

Margarete packs the large trunk. It's a lot of work! Everything they need fits inside.

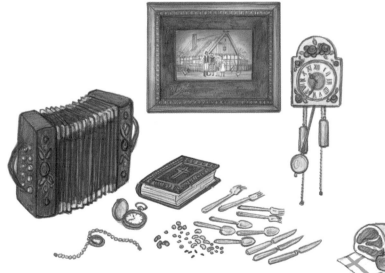

They are sure to remember the souvenir photo, the accordion, the family Bible, the pocket watch, Grandma Anna's necklace, some seeds, a clock, some silverware, and food for the trip.

The family is finally ready to go. Everyone takes only what they can carry.

The Journey Begins

An Expensive Voyage

Robert and Margarete worked hard to gather enough money for the steamship to America and a bit extra for starting their new lives. The trip costs 55 *thalers* for one adult and half that for a child, so the family's fare is 165 *thalers*. That's as much as a factory worker earns in six months.

Remembered Everything?

Robert obtained permission from the German government to emigrate and got a passport for his whole family. The newspaper published an article saying that the Peters family is leaving Germany and settling in Nebraska. Their taxes and debts have been paid. Now they face the toughest challenge: saying good-bye to family and friends forever.

Final Farewell

It is especially hard for Johannes and Dorothea to say good-bye to their grandparents. When Margarete's mother gives her a small bag of dirt from her garden so she will always have a little piece of home with her, Margarete begins to cry.

But through their tears, everyone wishes the family well. The priest gives them a blessing, and they climb into the waiting carriage to begin the journey.

They travel more than one hundred miles, which takes much longer than it would today. A carriage brings them to the train station, and they ride the train to the Elbe River. Then a ferry takes them across the river and on to Hamburg.

The announcers, merchants, and agents for the shipping company are doing a booming business. They offer everything from tinware to lodging to ship tickets—at prices much too high for some people.

The family will travel aboard the steamship *Teutonia*. But before they leave, the ship's cotton cargo is unloaded, and food and coal are brought on board. It's all hustle and bustle! Johannes and Dorothea watch everything with great curiosity. They never experienced such noise and commotion in their little town.

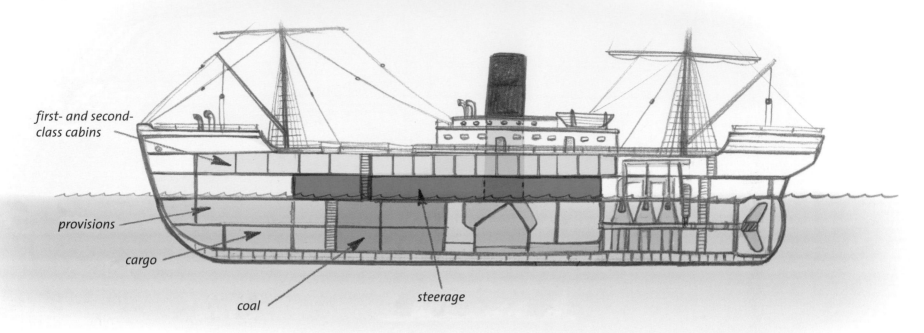

first- and second-class cabins

provisions

cargo

coal

steerage

The *Teutonia* is almost three hundred feet long and forty feet wide. With its steam engine, it can sail at ten knots (about eleven miles per hour). The sails help the ship go faster when the wind is good. The trip from Hamburg to New Orleans is more than five thousand miles and takes fourteen days. It would have been cheaper to take a sailing ship, but that voyage would have lasted six weeks.

Over the next two weeks, 310 people are crammed into double-stacked bunks in steerage. Beside the bunks are tables and benches for meals. The first- and second-class sections have cabins for 190 passengers, but those tickets cost a lot more.

16

The Voyage

Life in Steerage

Johannes and Dorothea were excited about the trip, but steerage is a lousy place to be. There is no light, no fresh air, and only a narrow bunk for the entire family. Another family sleeps in the bunk directly beneath them, and another next to them. The people aboard speak lots of languages. It starts to feel as if they have left their home for good.

At night Margarete hangs sheets around the bunk so they can have a bit of privacy. The chamber pots are emptied every day, but the air still stinks. It is hot and sticky. People get seasick and don't make it to the deck in time. And even worse, there are parasites on board. Bedbugs, fleas, and head lice—gross! Dorothea doesn't want to have to cut off her long hair.

Passing Time

Despite everything, Robert and a couple of the other men help keep spirits up by playing music. Robert plays his accordion, and everyone sings and dances until they are worn out. When a pregnant woman has her baby one night, they all get together to play her a little serenade.

Seeing the New World

As often as they can, Johannes and Dorothea go up on deck. Once they manage to stumble into the first-class section. The cabins have real furniture and portholes to let in the sunlight. They are soon discovered and shooed out, though.

Up on deck it's possible to see a long way over the ocean. One day Johannes and Dorothea see huge pink birds. Someone tells them they are called flamingos. They see another big bird called a pelican, which they later learn is on Louisiana's state flag. Soon the ship arrives in New Orleans.

From New Orleans to Omaha

In New Orleans

The Louisiana summer is hot and humid. The Peters family finally gets through passport control and medical examinations. Thank goodness none of them is being sent back to Germany because of illness.

A travel agent makes his way through the crowd. He speaks German, sells them tickets for the riverboat to St. Louis, and finds them a place to stay for the night. Everything is very expensive. Johannes and Dorothea look around in amazement.

On the Mississippi

The next leg of the journey lasts four days aboard the *Princess*. This time the family has their own cabin. The riverboat steams along the winding Mississippi River past elegant villas surrounded by shade trees. Some of the houses have been destroyed in the recent Civil War, which ended in 1865. Former slaves have been free for four years, but many still work on cotton plantations.

In St. Louis, Missouri, German immigrants have founded the German Society. The group helps newcomers. Someone there advises the Peterses to take the new Union Pacific Railway to Omaha, Nebraska. The train takes only one day to make the 450-mile trip.

In Omaha, Brown's General Store sells everything that settlers need. The building is packed full of sacks, crates, barrels, and shelves. Robert is having trouble remembering English words, but Margarete is paying close attention to the new names for the items they buy.

At the cattle market Robert and Johannes inspect two oxen. They are cheaper than horses and can easily pull a covered wagon. Robert also plans to have them pull his plow later.

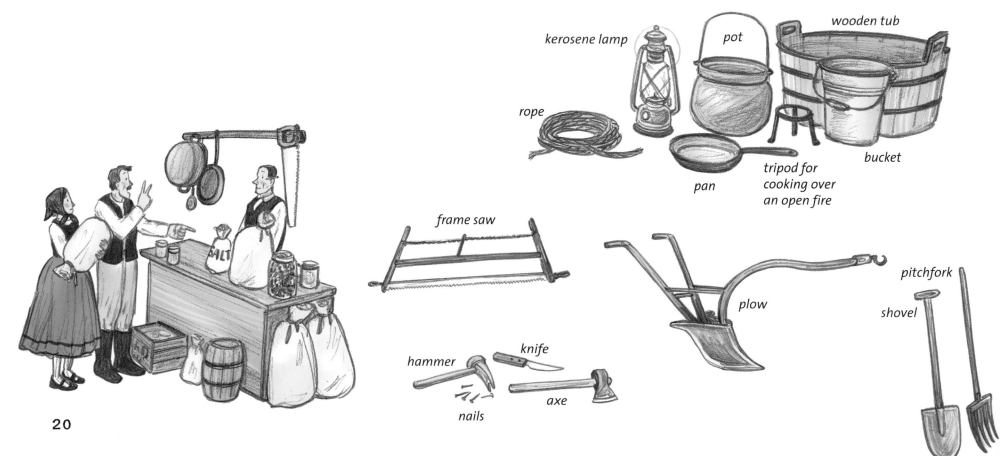

kerosene lamp

pot

wooden tub

rope

pan

tripod for cooking over an open fire

bucket

frame saw

plow

pitchfork

shovel

hammer

knife

axe

nails

20

From Omaha to New Steinberg

A City Full of People

In Omaha the Peterses encounter all sorts of people, from soldiers to Chinese railroad workers. Prospectors are making their way west, cowboys are loading their cattle onto freight trains bound for Chicago, and settlers are organizing wagon trains.

After a lot of asking around, they find the land office. Here they are given a square of land, marked with a number. They learn the location of their new property and that the next wagon train will leave in two days.

Traveling with the Wagon Train

The Peters family can hardly wait. Eighty families, each with their own wagon, follow the experienced wagon master along the path of the new railroad. This route offers protection from clashes with the Native Americans living on the prairie because the railroad tracks are guarded by soldiers.

They travel for ten long days. It is a tough journey. Everyone is anxious and worried. People fight about small things. But the trek also brings the settlers together. They will be neighbors when they arrive and will need to depend on each other. There are many Germans in the wagon train, but also people from Scandinavia, Switzerland, Ireland, and England. Johannes and Dorothea are delighted that there are other children. It helps them get over missing their old friends so much. The settlers are lucky and make it to their destination without any problems.

Finally There!

On the Vast Prairie

The little town near the Peterses' land is called New Steinberg. It was founded twelve years before by Germans and has about nine hundred residents, a church, a bank, a school, and many businesses. Soon the train station will be finished. Settlers come to shop or to sell their harvests. After a bit of searching, Robert and Margarete find out the location of their new property. They have no trouble communicating in New Steinberg because most people speak German.

The family has more than 150 acres, just for them! The plot is square—a half mile long on each side. The Peterses are more than a half mile away from their closest neighbor, but they know that everyone will help each other.

A Chance for Everyone

The Homestead Act, signed into law by President Abraham Lincoln in 1862, governs the process of dividing land among settlers. Most important, it gives immigrants a chance for a new beginning as farmers and ranchers. The law also says that the rented land will belong to the settlers after five years if they cultivate it successfully.

Robert and Margarete want to own their land. By the light of the kerosene lamp, Robert writes in the family Bible how happy they are to be in the United States. They have been traveling for almost two months and have come more than six thousand miles.

Everyone is exhausted, but they are healthy and can get to work right away.

First the family needs a house. Wood for a log cabin is too expensive, but the prairie offers other possibilities. The family cuts blocks of sod and stacks them on top of one another to make walls. The roots of the tough prairie grasses will hold the walls together. The walls offer good protection from the wind and weather. Sod is put on the roof as well.

When spring arrives the family gets busy working the fields. Margarete is pregnant, but she still helps. She plants fruit trees and digs a big bed for beans and other vegetables, using the seeds they brought from Germany. Johannes helps her. Robert plows to prepare the field for planting grain, fixes fences, and builds a bigger shed for the animals. Dorothea tends to the cow and the chickens and makes sure they don't run away.

1870: The First Year on the Farm

First Success

The family harvests a grain crop the first summer. Johannes and Dorothea stay home from school to help. Robert hires a field hand to get all the work done. If everything keeps going this well, they will be able to afford more cows and horses, full-time field hands, and maybe even a housekeeper. Maybe someday they'll get a steam-powered tractor!

Robert and the neighbors plan to buy farm machinery together, but it will be a while until they can afford that.

A Startling Encounter

In the middle of the harvest, the family is startled by some Native Americans riding by. Dorothea immediately runs and hides in the field. The family knows that other settlers have been attacked in the past. But they don't need to fear the Pawnee, who have signed treaties with the US government to leave settlers in peace.

It would be more dangerous if the Native Americans were Lakota. They are still known to attack settlers. The Lakota agreed that settlers could use the land, but they did not realize how much their lives would change. Now they can no longer follow buffalo herds, build housing on good hunting grounds, or freely hold their tribal gatherings. Suddenly there are farms, fences, barns, and settlers in the way. Native peoples' territories are becoming smaller and smaller, and so they try to defend themselves.

Truly at Home!

New Names

In the fall Margarete and Robert invite their best friends and neighbors to their new wooden house. Gudrun (from Sweden) and Holly (from England) are overjoyed at the Peterses' new baby, Henry. He is the first true American in the family. Gudrun and Margarete know enough English now to understand Holly, even though she talks very fast. For the children the new language is no problem at all. Dorothea and her best friend—Holly's daughter Betty—share their secrets in English.

Holly decides that the Peterses' names are much too long, so she gives them new ones: Margarete becomes Maggy, Robert becomes Bob, Johannes becomes John, and Dorothea becomes Dotty. Even their last name is pronounced differently in English, with a longer "e" sound. "That's just how it sounds in English," Holly tells them. Now they feel as though this place is really home.

Good Friends

Bob and John Peters go out to the barn with neighbors Björn and Jack to look at their newly purchased horse. Bob won't have to do everything on foot now. Maggy lets the horse pull the wagon when she has to go into town. John and Dotty are excited to learn how to ride. Who could have imagined all of this just one year ago?

28

29

Almost 150 Years Later

Life Goes On

Bob and Maggy were very successful. After five years, in 1874, they earned the deed to their property. Bob and Maggy's grandchildren worked hard, too, and their children were able to buy even more land. During the stock market crash in 1929 and 1930, a lot of farmers gave up. But the Peters family stayed on the farm.

Five generations built up the farm, making it bigger. Today, Tom Peters lives in the wooden house with his wife, Kim. He owns almost one thousand acres, has his own farm machinery, and employs lots of people to help him. The house has grown, too, and the city of New Steinberg is hardly recognizable. Forty-two thousand people live here now. Only a very few speak German anymore. Tom is one of them. He learned as a child from his family and passed it on to his own children.

What Was It like Back Then?

Tom and Kim's children go to school in New Steinberg. Daniel is nine years old and attends elementary school, and Olivia, who is twelve, is at the middle school. Olivia is working on a school project about the history of immigrants. She asks her parents a lot of questions. She knows the old photo hanging above the fireplace well. Olivia's father told her that the photo is of her grandparents' grandparents, Grandpa Bob and Grandma Maggy, and their children in front of their house in Germany. But when did they move to Nebraska? How did they get here? Tom tells her what he knows. The stories make everyone curious, so they decide to travel to Germany that summer.

Tom's family wants to find the old house in the photo. They hope it's still standing.

Olivia can hardly believe her luck! In the old trunk in the attic, there are treasures for her project: tickets for a steamship, old linens, a tiny sack of dirt, an old pocket watch, and lots of other items.

The most important thing is the family Bible, in which Bob wrote his hopes and dreams. If only he knew how many of them had come true.

The whole family does research online and borrows books from the library to learn more. Where will they need to go in Germany? They know the name of the village, but borders have changed and it isn't in the province of Hanover anymore—now it is in Lower Saxony. They are going to make their journey by ship, the way Bob, Maggy, John, and Dotty did long ago.

Finally they are ready to board the ship to Hamburg.

33

Sausage and beer are not everyone's favorite.
But there is lots of American food in Germany:
bagels, doughnuts, spare ribs, steak, and hamburgers.

Like many tourists the
Peterses collect souvenirs,
write postcards, and go on
tours of Hamburg.

In a little village in Lower Saxony, they find the old house
still standing! Olivia sees it first.

There It Is!

Coming Full Circle

This house is where Robert, Margarete, Johannes, and Dorothea began their journey so many years ago. It's really still there—freshly renovated and painted. After almost 150 years, Tom, Kim, Olivia, and Daniel are standing in the same spot where their relatives once stood.

Memories

An old woman watches them curiously. Tom asks her if she would take a photo of them in front of the house. When he tells her that his last name is Peters, she remembers her great-grandfather telling her about the Peters family. Like so many Germans, they dared to cross the ocean to America. Her great-grandfather was six years old when they left and was very impressed.

Discovering Germany

At first Germany seems strange to Tom and his family. But they know that Bob and Maggy must have felt the same way in the United States. It seems as if there are almost as many cultures living together in Germany as there are back home in the United States. The Peters family knows they will visit again.

35

In the Peterses' house in Nebraska, a second photo now hangs over the fireplace, right next to the one of Robert, Margarete, and their children.

Published by Charlesbridge
85 Main Street
Watertown, MA 02472
(617) 926-0329
www.charlesbridge.com

First published in Germany in 2013 by Julius Beltz GmbH & Co. KG, Beltz Verlag,
Postfach 10 01 54, D-69441 Weinheim/Bergstraße, Werderstr. 10, D-69469 Weinheim,
Germany, as *In Die Neue Welt: Eine Familiengeschichte in Zwei Jahrhunderten*.
Copyright © 2013 Beltz & Gelberg in der Verlagsgruppe Beltz · Weinheim Basel

Library of Congress Cataloging-in-Publication Data
Raidt, Gerda, author.
   [In die neue Welt. English]
   In the new world: A family in two centuries/Gerda Raidt and Christa Holtei;
translated by Susi Woofter.—First US edition.
      p. cm.
   "First published in Germany in 2013 by Beltz & Gelberg."
   ISBN 978-1-58089-630-6 (reinforced for library use)
   ISBN 978-1-60734-783-5 (ebook)
   ISBN 978-1-60734-782-8 (ebook pdf)
1. Peters family—Juvenile literature. 2. German Americans—Biography—Juvenile
literature. 3. Immigrants—United States—Biography—Juvenile literature.
4. Farmers—Nebraska—Biography—Juvenile literature. 5. Germany—Biography—
Juvenile literature. 6. Germany—Emigration and immigration—Juvenile literature.
7. United States—Emigration and immigration—Juvenile literature. I. Holtei, Christa,
author. II. Woofter, Susi, translator. III. Title.
E184.G3R215 2015
973'.0431—dc23   2013049025

Printed in China
(hc) 10 9 8 7 6 5 4 3 2 1

Display type set in Periodico Display by Eduardo Manso
Text type set in The Sans by Luc as de Groot
Color separations by Jade Productions, Hong Kong
Printed by Jade Productions in Heyuan, Guangdong, China
Production supervision by Brian G. Walker
Designed by Diane M. Earley